"I was deeply touched by this poetic and magical fable. The story of ~~Prince ~~ anguish and despair of growing up in a family where you don't fit in. The Prince is one of these children—fallen far from the parental tree. His struggle with bipolar disorder makes him feel even more out of sync with his family. But fortunately, he meets a peasant girl who turns out to be a fairy princess who helps guide him to find his true self. This book gives hope to anyone dealing with a mental health condition in a neglectful, unaware family. I urge everyone grappling with mental illness and their loved ones who are affected by it to read this book. Weiler lets everyone know that a sweet recovery may be in store for them too."

Sharon S. Dunas, LMFT

President, National Alliance on Mental Illness, Westside Los Angeles

NAMI San Mateo County
1650 Borel Place, Suite 130
San Mateo, CA 94402
Phone: (650) 638 0800
www.namisanmateo.org

The Anguished Prince

A Fairytale in Reverse

By Peter D. Weiler

Acknowledgements

For this novella, I am indebted to Mary Victoria Elder, and Janis Hunt Johnson, without whom it would not be possible.

Dedication

The style of this story is for young adults, a very important population from 15 to 25. It is in this age range that many are first beset by mental illnesses such as bipolar, depression, schizophrenia, and many others. If you, dear reader, do not have a mental illness, perhaps you have a friend, a classmate, or a relative who does. Young adults need a way to process these maladies; and this fable, in a whimsical way, deals with these serious subjects.

However, this tale is also for people who are older than 25. Mental illness strikes people of all ages. In addition, people of any age may have someone with a mental condition in their lives.

In addition, this novella is not only for those suffering from mental sickness. There are many people who face other challenges: chronic physical illness, learning disabilities, bullying, divorce. They may look at the characters of this work overcoming tremendous odds and say, "I can do this, too."

Please read this short novel several times. There are many layers to it, which will be revealed with each reading. It was written, intentionally, in a romantic, light, simple-languaged and mischievous manner, and covers many difficult topics other than just bipolar. And the factors just mentioned, along with a gripping plot, make the work an intriguing page-turner that can be read in one delightful sitting.

Finally, at the end of the day, it is a beautiful love story. For that reason, anybody who is in love or wants to be in love can enjoy and identify with it thoroughly.

Wishing you Love and Hope,

Peter

Caveat: This novella deals with serious medical, psychological, and psychiatric illnesses and conditions. It is not meant to prescribe any clinical solutions to any of them. Please see and follow the directions of a licensed medical doctor, therapist, and psychiatrist.

Chapter 1: Prince Tim in the Palace

Once upon a time, in the palace of the most powerful Island Kingdom in the world, lived a prince named Timothy, nicknamed Tim. By the age of five, his highly observant family members realized that he was not smart, handsome, or brave, and they all expressed their disappointment in him in their own unique ways.

When he was born, however, there was much joy in the palace, for the heir of the throne was begotten. Tim grew up fairly content, playing many games with his only friend Johnnie, a confirmed redhead with freckles and green eyes who, being a joyful and rascally kid, was full of shenanigans. *Johnnie tastes like red licorice because his hair is red, and he sweetens my life*. One day, though, Johnnie's family moved back to the nearby Western Island, and Tim turned sad and lonely.

On his tenth birthday, life changed dramatically, for his brother Cornelius was born. It was then that he started stuttering badly.

The queen, Marra, stopped spending what little time she had spent with him before, and turned completely neglectful. As a result, other than Paul—a kind guard in his fifties—Tim lost the ability to connect with people altogether.

"Ma ma ma mother, wha why di did you ha have ano another ki kiii kid?"

"I wanted another child. Just deal with it and stop stuttering, already. You are driving me up the wall."

The queen had a pale complexion, never smiled or wore cosmetics, and she dressed in white clothes only, because attracting the king meant nothing to her. *The queen tastes like the plain ice cream flavor vanilla, though rancid.*

What scared Tim the most was something Paul once revealed, which was that a girl with extremely limited intellectual abilities, whom the queen neglected horribly, was born before him. Eventually, that girl died, and the queen did not even cry.

Instead of becoming sad, she turned colder, bitterer, and more unfeeling. He often wondered if she had his brother, because she considered him—Tim—to be a mistake too. There was no telling how he would have ended up without a female figure in his life—until a very special person came along—a peasant girl named Emma. But I am getting ahead of myself.

Instead of being home, his father, King James, was always preoccupied with fighting wars or meeting with the financial advisors. He had a somber face, with a thick, charcoal-black beard that reached way past the heart and covered it quite well, and a thick moustache of the same color. His black eyebrows were exceedingly bushy and scary.

"Wha wha why do do don't you e e ever pa pa play wi wi with me?"

"I have a kingdom to run. When I was ten, I excelled in literature, music, and drama, and did not play kids' games or read kids' books. How will you be the king when you grow up?! Just be happy I put food in your mouth, and stop whining!"

The king's constantly pointing out Tim's flaws filled him with ever-present shame, which corroded his inner psyche like a corrosive acid. He was also confused about the irate glares he got, from the king, whenever he cried. Tim thought that he was unlovable, and he had absolutely nothing good to say about himself.

But his father's anger was the most hurtful. Although he never hit Tim, the rage was so grievous, there was no telling what to expect next. *The king tastes like the ice cream flavor dark chocolate with those nasty, hard, dark chocolate bits. I like milk chocolate, but the dark chocolate is harsh, and the chunky bits almost break my teeth.*

Tim was a frightened child. He had five recurring nightmares: living in the palace, being the king, fighting in wars, enduring the king's wrath, or training for battle. He would wake up from them with a pounding heart in a cold sweat. And going back to sleep was a challenge.

His maternal grandmother, Eva, a hideous woman with curly black hair, also lived with them. When she, a cold and critical woman, saw how ordinary Tim was, she said cruel things. "You'll never amount to anything."

"No no no ay ay I'm not! Ah, ah, I'll sh sh show you."

"No no no yu yu you wo wo won't," she imitated him, viciously. "You wet the bed every night, and the laundress has to wash the sheets daily." This was unbearable, and he would burst into tears, which just brought more ridicule.

She tastes like the ice cream flavor—no—ice cream is too good for her. She's more like those obnoxious lemon sour balls that are so tart, I always regret putting them in my mouth. Marra would hear the torment, but out of respect, and because of her own cold-heartedness, she never stood up for him. Tim felt betrayed all over the palace.

Finally, his mother's younger brother, Murdoch, resided in the palace, as well. He was a devious teenager, who although handsome, looked unwholesome. With a mouth sporting half a smile, like a vulture ever-ready to prey on a defenseless hare, he was verbally and emotionally abusive.

Murdoch constantly imitated Tim's stutter and poked fun at his bedwetting. But one day, he crossed the line. It was a Saturday afternoon and everybody was sleeping after a heavy meal, except for Tim and Murdoch.

Murdoch lured Tim to the balcony of the third floor of the palace, and placed him outside the fence of the balcony, dangling Tim by his feet upside down, for five whole minutes. It felt like an eternity. Afterwards, Tim was sternly cautioned not to tell a soul.

Tim was stumped, as it was obvious that Murdoch would have denied it, or, even if he—Tim—were believed, the queen would offer protection. Also, many families had their dirty little secrets, *especially* the royal family.

Paul the guard was the only one who could help. He was incensed at Murdoch's disgusting behavior. He decided that, although normally one should go to the authorities, since it would be futile, the uncle would have to be taken care of privately. So the next day, Murdoch was lured away and got a major hiding by Paul, with an assurance that nobody would believe that he—Paul—could have done it. The uncle was promised a severely painful beating if it were ever to recur.

Murdoch never bothered him again. But the fear that Tim had during those five minutes was *never* forgotten. *Murdoch is no type of food at all, but rather that stinky stuff that comes out of the body as a result of eating food.*

Tim disliked his parents, his grandmother, and his brother Cornelius. He hated Uncle Murdoch, and he hated being the prince. With tight stockings and tight shoes (to prevent running around freely), and a restrictive scratchy cravat, which felt like a noose, the palace felt like a dungeon, and he felt like a boy condemned to misery.

Luckily, though, Tim had two things going for him. Paul snuck in some commoner's clothes and shoes for him. And Tim had a "public" face. Visitors would say, "Oh wow, you look just like my nephew," or, "This is uncanny, but you look just like my neighbor's kid."

Tim's regular clothes and his "public" face turned out to be quite advantageous when that special peasant girl entered his life, because they could hang around together without suspicion. Tim's redemption from an undeserved life sentence, behind the walls of the palace, was just around the corner.

Chapter 2: Tim Meets Emma

One day, Tim, who was ten at the time, marched right out of the palace walls. Walking down the country trails, he saw an eleven-year-old peasant girl. Her name was Emma.

Emma was aware that the royalty was keen on maintaining the status quo. Her mother had to pay unjustified taxes to the kingdom. And peasants had no legal recourse.

Her neighbor was forced to work for the kingdom without pay. He could also be summoned for war, on just a day's notice, because a peasant's time and life were deemed dispensable.

But Emma was determined to remain cheerful and optimistic, and to help people who suffered. Ironically, the next person she would comfort was none other than Tim—the prince himself.

When Tim spotted her, she was preoccupied, gently playing with a monarch butterfly, watching it flutter, with all its grandeur, in yellow and orange hues. It suddenly escaped, and she ran into him.

"I'm sorry. Are you fine?"

Tim, being bashful, said nothing.

With a welcoming smile, extending her hand forward, she said, "Hi friend, I'm Emma. Nice to meet you."

"Oh, ha ha hi e e em Emma. M m m my ney ney name i i is ti ti Tim."

"Tim, you don't have to be afraid of me, or anything like that."

"Oh, that's a good thing. I'm very glad. Hey, how strange. I'm not stuttering anymore. It's nice to meet you, too." He finally shook her hand, which was soft like his pillow, and smooth, almost like the palace's white marble. Shaking a girl's hand for the first time was very pleasant. "Your hand is very warm. How come?"

"I'm happy, and that warms up the body."

This reminded Tim that he was scared and sad.

Emma, being intuitive, already knew this, due to the stutter and the cold hand. She also realized that he was a good soul, someone who would become a great person one day. "Do you live around here?"

"Nearby. And you?"

"Also nearby. Hey, wanna hang out? You seem like a cool kid. You probably get that a lot." She sensed that Tim was friendless, and that a positive practical joke was in order.

Nobody ever thought I was cool before. "Oh yeah," he lied, because who wants to contradict such an agreeable girl?

Emma was average-looking, with black hair and sparkling brown eyes, and she was about Tim's height. She wore a plain yellow peasant's dress and blouse—which were torn a bit—with a yellow sash, and simple worn-out girl shoes.

But with a captivating smile, a sky-blue hair ribbon, and a lovely amicable and charming character, she was beautiful to him. *Emma would be my favorite ice cream flavor—strawberry with mini white marshmallows.*

She saw that Tim was also average-looking. However, with his thick boyish black hair, eyelashes as long as a girl's, and his rare innocence, she found him attractive.

Every time their eyes met, his pupils got bigger, which showed his interest in—and affinity towards—her. He wore new commoner's clothes, just simple sturdy blue pants and a green cotton buttonless shirt, with short sleeves. They liked each other the moment they met.

Chapter 3: The Meadow

They walked together to a meadow. The palace had some nice grasslands, but this one was watered by the rain for free. It had poppies, with red petals and black insides, and purple irises, with yellow stripes. The sweet smell of nectar was intoxicating.

Tim saw a hummingbird sipping the nectar. It seemed so light, happy, and carefree that he was envious. *How I long to be a hummingbird and not be forced to eat the fancy palace food or be imprisoned there. Why must I be so sad and serious?*

And speaking of the palace, a harsh hot breeze was breathing down his neck, as though the king and queen were still watching. Unfortunately, even there, with his new friend, freedom was not at hand.

Suddenly, there was a rustle in the bushes.

"Shh…we have some lovely visitors. Please sit still," she whispered.

A regal, light-brown-and-white-speckled stag appeared, followed by a doe and her fawn. *Hmm…there's nothing special about the young one.*

"What a handsome child. Watch this." Emma breathed in and out rhythmically for a few minutes. The deer looked with curiosity, and approached.

She pet them all, but especially the fawn, saying, "Hi cutie, it's so nice to meet you." The little one licked her cheek.

Tim was astonished.

"Would you like to pet them?"

"Won't they run away?"

"They see us as their friends."

Tim petted the fawn, whose body was shivering. At first, it was scared, but slowly it rubbed against him and finally sat down.

"How does it feel to nurture something?" She asked, looking intensely into his eyes.

"It feels good. I can't think of anything else."

"I want you to remember this feeling."

"Why?" he asked with a blank stare.

"Never mind." *Tim is not ready for this yet*. Then, she gently passed her fingers through his hair. *You need nurturing, too.*

Eventually, the deer left the meadow.

Chapter 4: Emma's Secret, Girl Power, and the Sweet Bond

"How did you do that?! It was like magic."

"I meditated using all five senses. Since animals do this all the time, they thought I was one of them, and they weren't afraid. I read about it in a book from the library."

"But girls aren't allowed there."

"I have my ways. My mother sewed a boy's outfit with a hood. Mr. Brook, the librarian, is a friend. It's unfortunate that females are held back, in our kingdom, for no reason at all."

"I agree." And then it occurred to Tim that she was the first person whom he had connected with after Johnnie moved, and besides Paul.

"Meditation even helped me stop being ticklish. My older boy cousins foolishly think it's cool to bully girls around. They would tickle me mercilessly. I read that by meditating, taking twigs, and passing them under my arms and around my neck, I could eventually be completely immune to being tickled. The next time they tried to tickle me, they found out that it was futile. I was never bothered again."

"You really stood up for yourself."

"I had to. But I also stand up for my friends," she said, looking into his eyes, reassuringly. "But, please promise me you won't tell *anybody* about the books.

"In the olden days, various cultures bonded and promised things by drawing blood, and sucking it, and all kinds of nonsense. Let's think of a pleasant way to do so, like hugging."

And Emma gave Tim a hug. But she was not ready for what occurred next.

Tim started shaking uncontrollably, and sobbed bitterly.

"What's the matter, Tim?"

"My mother stopped hugging me altogether when my brother Cornelius was born, and I really miss it."

Poor Tim. How odd! she mused. "Then let me give you another one, and I won't let go." She embraced him until there was total calm, and she wiped away the tears. "I have to go home now; please walk me there." When they arrived at a small hut, Emma requested, "Can you please come visit me tomorrow at three in the afternoon?"

"Absolutely!"

Chapter 5: Three Surprises

That was the happiest day of Tim's life—so far anyway. He was comforted at knowing that Emma was older and smarter.

That night, for once, instead of nightmares, Tim had a pleasant dream. In it, both of them were nine years older, and they were getting married by a civil magistrate. There was no telling, though, whether or not the king and queen were there. He woke up, to his surprise, with dry sheets.

Tim never wet the bed, or stuttered, again. He decided to keep hiding the fact that he was the prince from her on purpose; he did not want special treatment. *Maybe she sees in me something that nobody else, including me, does,* he wondered.

Chapter 6: Tim at Emma's Hut and a Few Things that Bother Him

The next day, at thirty minutes past two in the afternoon, Tim walked out of the palace. Nobody even cared, but Emma would, and that was all that mattered.

At around three, he knocked on the door. A young woman answered, "Oh hi, Tim. I'm Emma's mom. Come on in. She said you're a very special person. Hey sweetie, your friend is here."

"Tim, I'm so glad to see you again." Emma gave him a big hug.

Tim was astounded. Emma was not shy at all in showing friendship publicly, and in front of her mother, at that. *Are all commoners this free-spirited? In the palace this would* never *happen.*

"Well, let me give you the royal tour."

Tim shuddered and winced with pain, at hearing the term "royal." Emma noticed it, but said nothing. "So this is the living room, kitchen, and dining room— all in one," she giggled.

Tim could not understand how people can live like that, and be so happy. "The door over there leads to my mom's bedroom, and this one goes to mine. Come on in." He was speechless. The room had only a little red desk, an orange chair, and a light-green closet. On the floor were white sheets, colored with light pink stripes, which contained something. "Here, let's sit on my beautiful bed." He was amazed because it felt as though it were stuffed with dry grass.

"Isn't it hard to sleep on this bed?"

"Oh, not at all; I love it—my bed, my room, my house, and even the outhouse—very much. I wouldn't exchange them even for the palace."

He trembled. *Did she know something?*

"Are you fine?"

"Yeah—just felt a little chill on my back."

But Emma was not buying it. *I'm not going to ask him about this further. He'll tell me when the time is right,* she decided.

"Where did you buy all this furniture?"

"We got the lumber for free from a lumber yard, which was going to toss it. My mother and neighbor built the furniture, by hammering the nails in the wood, and I painted it."

Tim was shocked. He never had to build or paint anything. Emma and her mother were very hard-working people, and Emma did everything to make a beautiful life for herself.

They went to the backyard, where there was a big thorn bush, pea plant, and some flowers. Emma picked two and gave them to him. "A yellow rose is a sign for Friendship. A yellow iris is a sign for Hope. Now we have them *and* the hug."

"Yeah, I guess," he said, pensively.

Why is Tim so sad and solemn, as though carrying the weight of the whole kingdom on his shoulders? It hurts me to see him that way.

Tim started to feel ever closer to Emma, for she really cared. But not being able to introduce her to his family caused much pain. The king and queen would not care that she was the only girl who brought joy into his life.

"I'm going home, Emma."

"Hey Tim, can you please invite me over sometime?" Emma requested, looking deeply into his eyes.

Tim looked at her sadly, and then stared at the ground. *I'm ashamed of being a prince.* "One day. But for now, if it's alright with you, let's meet at your home, or where we met originally."

"I'll meet you halfway, at three in the afternoon, at our regular spot," she said begrudgingly.

Tim started to walk to the palace. There had been a question that had been troubling him since he first met her. *Why does Emma like me so much?!*

Chapter 7: Three Years Later—Secrets

He saw her the next day, and the day after that. Days turned into weeks; weeks into months; and months into years. Emma was 14 and Tim was 13.

One day Emma said, "Do you want to play the secrets game? I'll tell you a secret, and then you'll tell me one. Here's mine: I'd like to become the librarian, when Mr. Brook retires."

"Wow, that's really cool. Nice game."

"Is there any secret you want to tell me?"

"No, I don't have any secrets."

But she knew that there was something he was too afraid of or too ashamed to reveal to her. *How I wish Tim would let me into his head, heart, home, and family.*

He went back to the palace, and Emma stood there, concerned and much frustrated.

Chapter 8: Tim and Emma Fall in Love

Days, weeks, months, and years passed by; Emma turned 17 and Tim 16. He started to develop deep feelings towards her.

One day, they walked to their beloved meadow and sat down. Emma took out a yellow rose, which had started turning red at the petals' edges, that she hid behind her dress, in the sash, and gave it to him. She looked at him, her head tilted coyly, and remarked, "Tim, you're a charming guy; I have very strong feelings for you."

"Like the ones I have for you?"

"Yeah, I've had them for some time. They're called love, and people who love each other, don't just tell each other, they show it." She came closer, and ran her fingers through Tim's thick black hair. Then, she took her yellow ribbon out, and let her black hair flow.

Tim was taken aback. He ran his fingers through her long, soft, thick, and lovely hair.

She caressed his cheeks and brought their lips together, and Tim got his first real kiss from the most gorgeous girl in the world, the only one who always cared about him—his best friend—Emma.

"Well, we're officially boyfriend and girlfriend now," she said.

They kept on doing things together, and hugging and kissing. Now, their hugs lasted a lot longer, and were closer and tighter; Emma initiated these times. When he asked her, she said that is what a boyfriend and girlfriend do. Tim was very pleased.

Chapter 9: Two Years Later—The Confrontation

Two years passed; Emma was 19, and Tim just turned 18. One day, he felt that it was the right time to ask the worrisome question, "Emma, why have you loved me all these years?"

"You were always gentle, and you respected the fact that, although I am a girl, I read and I'm smart. There is one more reason, but I can't say it now, because you need to grow into it, naturally. Tim, you *are* a very special man, and I'm honored to be your best friend, and girlfriend."

And for the second time, in front of Emma, Tim started sobbing uncontrollably.

"What's the matter, sweetie?"

"You've just said more kind things to me than I've heard in my entire life."

"What kind of parents do you have, Tim?! I *must* have a word with them! And I also need to see your home—now! No more secrets—understand?!" said Emma, furiously.

"Fine, Emma," said Tim, who calmed down instantly, as he has never seen her angry before. "I'll take you there."

Slowly, they approached the palace. "What's going on? Is this some kind of joke? I *need* to see your home!"

"It's straight ahead."

They walked together, till they reached the gate. Paul's friend—another guard at the palace—asked, "Your Highness Prince Tim, who is this person?"

"She's my girlfriend, Emma. Please open up."

"Yes, your grace."

When Emma saw that they were out of earshot from the guards, she slapped him across the face. "You're the *prince*?! I was such a good friend to you. Then we became boyfriend and girlfriend, and kissed. Even now, had I not insisted, you *still* wouldn't have told me the truth. What kind of man are you?!" And she burst out sobbing.

"Emma, I'm so sorry. It's just that I—"

"Just that you what?! I don't ever want to see you again," she cried and she ran out the front gate, still weeping, disappearing from view.

Paul came up to him, put his arm around his shoulder, and said kindheartedly, "Girl troubles, Tim?"

"Yes. I don't know why she's so mad."

"Tim, even though your girlfriend made an effort to walk far enough away, I've extra sharp hearing, and I caught everything. She's right to be upset with you. Nobody likes to be lied to, even if it's by omission. Women are especially prone to be sensitive to this. If you were dishonest about this, she may think you'll cheat on her."

"You're right. I did lie to her the entire time. Do you think our relationship is over?"

"Not necessarily. Give her some space. Take a few days, and think of how to explain yourself; she may take you back."

Tim hurried, ate quickly, and jumped into bed. But he could hardly sleep that night. Those awful nightmares just kept coming in full force, drenching him with cold sweat.

He waited for three days, walked out the front gate, and knocked on her door at three in the afternoon.

Chapter 10: The Resolution

Upon seeing him, Emma started crying. "Tim, why did you come here? Just to cause me more heartache?"

"Not at all, Emma. I just want five minutes of your time. If after that, you want me to, I'll be gone forever."

Emma, hurting, let him in.

"There were a few reasons I hid from you my real identity. I wanted to see if you liked me for who I am—just Tim—and not the prince.

"Also, the royal family allows the prince to befriend only the daughters of noblemen or other princesses. I don't even like them, as they're very stuck-up and superficial. I wanted to be with you, because you're smart, kind, and humble, which is why I had to pretend to be a commoner.

"Finally, we'd be greatly punished if we were found hanging out together."

"I'm glad you came here and explained. But the most important thing still bothers me. Since a prince must either marry a nobleman's daughter or a princess, I'll lose you forever."

"Oh, sweet Emma."

That's the first time I heard him use such language—interesting, she noticed.

"I never even wanted to be a prince, let alone the king. Everybody in the palace is so concerned with propriety, and royal manners. I just want to be a regular person, living outside of the palace, with the woman I love. And that woman is you—Emma."

"Tim, you're wholeheartedly forgiven, but I do want a guarantee you'll marry me; let's consummate our relationship. It is not a sin, regardless of what the canon of the church of the kingdom says. When two people become one in a committed, loving manner, *nothing* will tear them apart—not even the regal laws."

After walking hand in hand to the middle of the meadow, Emma disrobed and Tim followed suit. They made passionate love among the purple irises with yellow stripes; two white doves flew above. There was a cool breeze and their bodies warmed each other. And Tim realized that, this time, he was totally free.

Afterwards, they looked into one another's eyes, and smiled with elation and delight.

That night, instead of bad dreams, Tim saw them holding hands, going to the meadow, and making love again. He could also make out a scene where they were living in the same small home, leading a simple life, and even eating food with their hands.

In the morning, he realized that, after making love to Emma, he could never live in the palace or be the king, thoughts that had haunted him since birth and were manifested in the horrific nightly visions. Tim never had these kinds of nightmares again. But, he was about to have a horrible daymare, which would complicate both their lives, immensely.

Chapter 11: Tim's Extremely Sad Illness

The next day, Tim found an opened letter on his bed. It was from Johnnie's parents:

Dear Tim,

We know how much you and our Johnnie loved each other. We regret to inform you that he was run over by a horse and died. His death was immediate, and he did not suffer. Please be strong.

Grief-stricken, he went under the blanket, fully clothed, head under the pillow, sobbing uncontrollably. At four in the afternoon, the maid was shocked to see him in that state.

"Prince Tim, are you alright?"

He was silent.

Concerned, she ran to the king and queen, and informed them.

"Tim, you need to stop this nonsense. I see my soldiers perish in wars all the time. Man up, and go eat something," said the king, irately.

But Tim did not budge.

"He just wants us to feel sorry for him, just like always. Let us go," the queen said dryly.

Tim could not believe how, even now, these insensitive characters stayed in character.

The next morning the king was told, once again, that the prince was still in bed at four in the afternoon. "Get out of bed *now*!" yelled the king. But there was no movement. The king grabbed him violently and pulled him onto the floor.

Tim immediately crawled back into the bed.

"I will show you," bellowed the king, and he went to the bathroom sink, returning with a vessel filled with cold water, and spilled it on Tim.

This really jarred him. Getting splashed with cold water in bed is painful and shocking. And it feels undeserved—especially for one in his condition, and by a father like his. He got out of bed.

"You did not think I could do it—did you?!" yelled the king, victoriously.

But, Tim was so sad that, when the king left, he jumped right back into bed. People in that condition will do *anything* to block reality, including sleeping as much as possible.

The next morning, his parents were told that, once again, he had been in bed for a whole day—no showers, no grooming, and he had not eaten a thing.

"What is the matter, Tim?" asked the king, genuinely concerned.

"Things will never get better. No one can help me, and no one cares about me. I am going to go to Hell. I do not even want to live anymore."

The king was quite embarrassed, as one of Tim's assertions was true. He rarely had the time, or desire, to care about his son. But with all his toughness and power, hearing that Tim did not want to live anymore, caused the fortified wall, which had always surrounded his heart, to crack.

The king realized that help should come from an outside party, so the royal doctor recommended the best talk doctor in the kingdom, Dr. Bull, who also dispensed medicines—a talk medical doctor.

Chapter 12: Dr. Bull

The next day, Dr. Bull came to the palace. He was a humorless man, unless he was putting down a patient. He demanded extreme conformity—and he got it, as people feared him tremendously.

Tim had heard of this shady, callous person, who was unfortunately also a respected board member of the main hospital in the capital. He saw patients excessively, even when they were stable. Doctors of the same hospital constantly received needless referrals from him for bribes. People said that he entered the profession mainly for financial gain.

There was a newspaper which reviewed various businesses and professionals. Tim once read in it a horrible review about Dr. Bull, and was shocked to find out that Dr. Bull broke confidentiality by responding to the review, with specific details about the case, in order to defend his actions.

He cleared his throat, like many talk medical doctors, and said, "Ahem, so young man, you do not want to live. Is that right?"

"Yes. Hey, Dr. Bull, how are you?" he asked, trying to cheer himself up, and build rapport, at the same time.

"Young man, I am your doctor, not your friend," Dr. Bull yelped.

"Yes Sir." *Wow, this is a great conversation starter. And you are a bully!*

"What makes you not want to live?"

"My childhood friend Johnnie died."

"Will this bring him back? Is that what he would have wanted?"

"All I know is that I do not want to live."

"Why do you not eat? You will lose weight and get sick."

"I have no appetite. I wish that I will get sick. That way, at least I will feel something. Right now I do not feel anything."

"And how does that make you feel?"

Is this guy for real?! I just told him I don't feel anything. He went to medical school for this?! "I am not sure."

"I hear that you are not doing anything. Some people get really sad so that they can be lazy."

"But most idle people feel pretty good, because they do not do much. I do not follow."

"Do not be fresh with me." It was important for him to maintain leverage over Tim; otherwise, he—Dr. Bull—would grow nervous.

"I am sorry."

"Why will you go to Hell?"

"I do not know; I just *feel* that I am going there."

"Why do you think you are hopeless? You are going to be the king one day."

Tim, extreme sadness notwithstanding, almost burst out laughing. Being the king was a good reason *not* to have hope. "I cannot explain it. What do you suggest?"

"Just be happy. You have the basic necessities for living. You are not a peasant and…"

"But—"

"Do not interrupt me, young man."

This man is so full of himself. "Fine."

"Take four of these in the morning and four at night." He put a huge bottle of pills on Tim's desk. "I will be back tomorrow. And stop being so sad. Look at what you are doing to your parents!"

"Wait a minute. I will see you twice a week, not every day."

"Usually, I refuse to treat people like you," he said, "but since you are the king's son, I will tolerate it."

I can't believe this doctor is maintaining such a distance and demanding so much respect. "And I will be happy!" he taunted him and grinned victoriously.

Dr. Bull belittled Tim's complaints about the medicines' side effects. A doctor must be able to put himself in the patient's shoes, and to care, but that was not the case here. And when poor Tim, who got no activity, exercise, or personal care, barely improved, Dr. Bull told the king that Tim did not want to get better.

Chapter 13: Emma Finds Out, and Her Brilliant Plan

All this time, Emma was worried sick; Tim had not come to see her for a whole month. She was determined to find out what was wrong.

It was a stormy and thunderous night. Whenever lightning struck, the guards ran away from their posts and hid under nearby trees, out of fear. Emma took advantage and snuck in.

She moved furtively throughout the palace, slinking from room to room. Finally, groans of Tim tossing and turning in agony were heard. The room was dark. She got on her knees, and ran her fingers through Tim's hair.

"Emma, what are you doing here? Do you realize what will happen to you, if you're caught?"

"I don't care about all that. Please tell me what's going on. I'm really concerned."

Tim told her everything, and how he still did not want to live anymore.

Emma wept quietly, but she thought of an ingenious idea. "Tim, you need extra assistance—the human touch that doctors can't, won't, and don't want to give.

"Tell your parents that you want a companion, and ask them to place advertisements. I'll show up right away, declaring loyalty, and a willingness do it for free."

"Wait, so you'll say that you're sooo faithful to them, after we made love? You're funny Emma," and they both laughed. "I haven't laughed in a month," said Tim reflectively.

"That's because I'm back with you, Tim; I won't abandon you, my love," and she tenderly kissed his forehead.

He hugged her and begged, "Please steal out of the palace quickly. I'll get on with your plan, first thing tomorrow morning."

The king agreed that it was a great idea, and he was actually surprised that Tim came up with it all on his own.

Chapter 14: Emma the Companion

The next day, a young woman showed up immediately, with a flier in her hand. The king was impressed but had some reservations.

"Tim, would she be good enough? After all, she is just a woman—and a peasant, at that."

"We should at least give her a chance." Emma and Tim did their best not to laugh. They saw that even in his dismal condition, Tim still had a sense of humor.

"Ahem, wait," protested Dr. Bull. "I am already helping him enough." His inadequacy was exposed, and he was being upstaged by a poor peasant woman— all too much for his ego.

"Oh no, Tim is my son. He will get whatever assistance is necessary," asserted the king, annoyed.

The doctor, turning red with embarrassment and rage, excused himself, before saying anything that would put him in jeopardy.

"I will let my advisors take over."

"So, peasant woman, we will pay you very little."

"The royalty are already doing so much for us filthy peasants that I will do it for free."

"This peasant really knows her place on the food chain. When can you start?"

"Right away, Sires. The prince has suffered enough, already."

"She has a good work ethic, too," said the advisors, who worked very little. "You may come and go as you please, and avail yourself of all of the palace's resources."

"Thank you. Prince Tim, you need to shower and groom."

He followed her instructions.

"Let's eat breakfast; you've lost a lot of weight."

"But, I'm not hungry."

"You need to eat anyway. What will it be?"

"If anything, then it should be runny scrambled eggs with fried onions, fried shallots, and fried-chopped, hard-dried salami sticks."

"That's perfect. Exotic food is easier to eat."

Emma placed their order, and within ten minutes, the maidservant came with a huge tray.

The food was so delicious that he gobbled it. "It's very tasty. I'll have seconds."

"But not thirds. You'll be drowsy, and we have things to do."

He ate another plate.

"Let's go to the courtyard. You need fresh air, sunlight, and exercise."

"May I please hold your hand?"

"Of course."

"Emma, your hand is as soft, smooth, and warm as it was on the first day we met."

Emma gently slipped her hand away from his, and she squirmed with discomfort.

His mother always told him that only royalty have such hands, because they do not work, whereas the dirty peasant women have rough hands, because they do hard manual jobs.

But his parents were wrong about peasants, especially Emma who outsmarted them cold. She had figured out how to be with their son in the palace, something which was prohibited even outside of it.

The air was fresher than that of the staid room where he had been staying in bed for a month. They reached the pond, and sat on a bench. "Look intently at the pond, the golden fish, and the lilies. Listen to the water flowing from the fountain. Doing both these things is relaxing and healing."

Tim grabbed her hand again, to feel reassured. Tim's cold, sad hands, warmed up in Emma's, and the rays of the sun made him happier. "How much I want to kiss you, dear Emma."

"I know that, but it doesn't feel right to me," she said and, once again, softly withdrew her hand. "Don't worry; it won't be long till you get better, and things will go back to where they were before." But secretly, she was glad, because Tim looked forward to a pleasurable activity, which was a sign of recovery. "Let's walk in the orchards."

She reached up, felt several of the fruits, picked a big, round, ripe orange persimmon, and gave it to Tim. He sensed the sweet, succulent, juicy smoothness of its flesh on his tongue. He bit into it so quickly, that it made a loud squirting sound. Emma's red blouse was sprayed.

Tim then realized that Emma was very meticulous in feeling out, and particular about examining, several fruits, before procuring that one, because when a persimmon is not ripe, it tastes sandy, and leaves a horrible aftertaste. This was symbolic of the way that she always protected him from anything unsavory.

"Let's sit on this patch of grass, and please tell me more about Johnnie— what he was like and the things you did together."

"Johnnie was a funny, cheerful, and happy-go-lucky kid, with flame-red hair, freckles, and green eyes. He was my only friend who was my age, and we played many games together. He made up silly songs that didn't even rhyme, he always exaggerated, and he jumped into puddles after heavy rains, splashing people. He never wore socks, and he whistled really loudly, almost making people deaf."

"Like this?" asked Emma, and let one out.

"Exactly! When did you learn how to whistle like that?!"

"As kids, it was a way to keep our spirits up. It sounds like Johnnie contributed greatly to your happiness, as a child."

"Very much. Somehow, we clicked. When his family moved back to the Western Island, I turned sad. Then you came along, and happiness returned. But when he died, all the good memories hit me, like a ton of bricks, and the horrible sadness appeared. Do you think people go to Heaven after they die? Where's Johnnie now?"

"I don't believe in Heaven in the religious sense—a place where there's no eating, drinking, playing, having friends, or making love. That's boring, so that is more like Hell. I believe that when a person dies, they return back to earth to live a good happy life, once more, even if we never see them again."

"It sounds like you believe that Johnnie is still singing silly songs without rhymes, telling exaggerated stories, splashing people with mud, whistling loudly, and wearing sandals without socks and running around with dirty feet."

"Either that, something just as good, or even better," Emma smiled.

"Thank you for listening to me, and understanding me, as opposed to shaming me, Emma."

"Of course, my…." Emma stopped herself short. "But talking to the doctor is important, so he can give you the right medicines and at the right amount, by seeing your improvement. I need to go home, now. I'll see you tomorrow."

The next day, Tim was ready.

"Let's go to the royal lake."

The lake water was clear and absolutely still.

"So, do you want to learn how to skip stones on water?"

"Really?! I didn't even know that was possible."

"Watch me closely." She picked up a smooth round stone and explained how to hold it, and how to toss, it. "Here, I'll do it, and you count."

Tim counted six. "That's amazing. My turn now."

She counted three. "Awesome, that's great for the first time."

"Can you top yourself?"

"Let's see," she said innocently.

Tim counted nine. "Hey, you got better."

"Thanks." That was the second positive practical joke she played on him. Emma could have skipped it around 70 times. "Now, your turn again."

He skipped it five times and was delighted. "You know, Emma, this game is symbolic. A stone is much heavier than water, and yet, with finesse, it can be lighter. It's like my problems. They, too, can be made lighter, if handled properly."

"Great insight, Tim. How do you feel now?"

"Much better. My problems have faded."

"I'm glad." Emma knew that although every method they utilized was important, so was the power of distraction—especially a new fun game. In addition, Tim learned an easy new skill, and that helped, too.

They played games every day. Of course, Emma always let him win, because engaging in competitive sports was risky. If he were to lose, it would demoralize him further.

Days, weeks, and months went by, and Tim's mood and appetite eventually improved, and the color returned to his face. But an ominous phase was about to commence.

Chapter 15: Tim's Too Happy–Too Sad Malady

One day, Emma noticed in Tim truly disturbing behaviors.

"Emma, Emma," Tim spoke excitedly, and with exaggerated bodily motions. "You're not going to believe this, but I only slept for four hours last night, and I'm not even tired. I invented a machine that would enable people to travel through time. Even if only half the world would buy it, I'll be the world's richest man. The food yesterday was great; charred beef is delicious. Going to the capital and buying expensive antiques sounds good. I've never felt better in my life. We can leave the palace tonight, and travel the world for the next ten years, with all the money my invention will make. Last night, our future mansion was right in the middle of the room."

Emma realized that Tim's illness had flipped from the truly sad illness to the rarer Too Happy–Too Sad sickness. The latter was more dangerous for two reasons. There was no known treatment in the medical community, and the person would inevitably get so out of hand, an indefinite stay in an insane asylum would be the only option.

But Emma remembered a book she had read that told about how 50 years earlier, such an ill person accidentally drank water at a special well, containing unusual salt deposits, and miraculously got better. From then on, they would take these desperately sick people to that well, and have them drink a cup a day.

Unfortunately, only natural healers knew about it, and very few people ever got

help.

If the person had the too-happy condition for a long time, then his recovery

would be followed by a long period of deep sadness. But since she caught Tim on

the first day, the hope was that the exceedingly sad part would be brief.

The book she had read gave its word, though. Sufferers would have to drink

the special well water, every day, for the rest of their lives, or the malady would

return. There were no exceptions—ever!

"Tim, rather than having extreme sadness only, you are in the too-happy

phase of a more dangerous condition called the Too Happy–Too Sad sickness.

You're not sleeping enough, yet have boundless energy. You talk non-stop, about

unrelated ideas. You're displaying poor judgment with spending money, and

you're seeing things that aren't there. Finally, you have unrealistically grand ideas

of what you're capable of accomplishing. I'm really worried about you."

"Well, worry about yourself!" he snapped at her.

And he's displaying bad temper, too. This is alarming. "Tim, please hear me

out. Don't you realize how everything is the exact opposite now? That's the definition of the too-happy state. Worst of all, your anger is dangerous, in general, and it is hurting my feelings."

"You're just jealous that I'm the greatest inventor in the world, as opposed to a mere peasant."

"How insensitive of you." Emma started weeping for herself, but for him, too. "Regular medicine has no treatment for this, but I can help."

"No thanks!"

Emma empathized with his skewed reasoning. The refusal to take medicine, according to the book, was nearly universal among the sufferers. The good feelings are so enjoyable, that taking care of the condition makes no sense to them. Almost anybody with that temptation would fall for it. The ill people think that everybody *else* is out of their minds.

Emma realized that tough love was in order, because he was becoming a threat to everyone, including himself. "Tim, I care very much, but there are limits. If you jump off a cliff, I'm not going to jump after you."

"But you were always my friend."

"You're not being a friend by refusing treatment, and by worrying me half to death."

"And we made love."

"You think you can soften me up by using guilt, you little manipulator?!" said Emma with feigned contempt.

"I think you're just trying to trick me into taking the medicines, in order to make the wonderful feelings disappear."

Emma realized that the whip had to be cracked, as a last resort. She decided to give Tim the ultimatum, just like they did long ago when the special water was discovered, and a combatively ill person would absolutely refuse to drink it.

She stared in his eyes, lowered her voice in the most threatening tone, and said, "Listen, if you don't cooperate and become compliant, I'm leaving for good."

"Well…."

"Alright, Tim, have a good life." She started for the door.

"Wait, please don't leave. If I take the medicines, will you stay with me?"

"Of course. But, you have to promise me to get treated."

"I don't want to lose you. So what's your plan?"

"For one thing, you must tell the talk medical doctor nothing about all this, or he'll commit you to an asylum immediately. Keep it short and sweet. 'Yes doctor, no doctor.' I'll be back with the medication first thing tomorrow morning."

Emma walked out of the palace. When all alone, she cried bitterly, and said, "Why must my poor Tim suffer so much? He didn't bring it on himself." And quietly added, "I'm sorry I had to go down hard on you today—there simply was no other choice."

She knew that for the Too Happy–Too Sad illness, the treatment was less talk, with more medical attention. The local natural healer was a friend of hers, and there had to be a special well, nearby.

He said that there was one about a half an hour's ride on a horse. He even lent her his stallion, a map, and two huge jugs, in order to fill a week's worth.

Emma had the chef make a concoction of half a tall glass of freshly squeezed orange juice, the special well water, and sugar, so that Tim could withstand the taste. The chef also made a tall glass of juice for her, as well.

"Here you go. The medicine is mixed with freshly squeezed orange juice and sugar."

They hung together some more, and Tim drank the potion every morning. Two weeks later, his bodily movements were steadier, and his speech was slower. "How is your sleep, my dear?"

"Six hours. The medicine is slowing me down. I don't like it."

That's the whole idea, sweetie.

"And I have to drink much more water, and go to the bathroom more often, which is annoying."

"I'm so sorry, Tim. The salt in the medicine dehydrates the body."

"I also have a tremor in the hands."

"Yeah, I've noticed that too, my love, but it's better than the alternative."

Two weeks later, Tim confessed to sleeping eight hours a night, again.

"Are you still going to be the greatest inventor?"

"Oh no, not at all," he said, embarrassed. "I'm just like I was before."

"And that's good enough for me," she smiled, and hugged him affectionately. Although Emma was in a different capacity now, ever since the too-happy condition, the rules were slightly bent, because it was so troubling, and the love for Tim was so great.

The signs of Tim's too-happy phase finally disappeared. Emma knew that the punishing sadness would start immediately, just not nearly as long, or as intensely, as before.

Chapter 16: Back to Extreme Sadness

The next day, Tim was back in bed, crying despairingly. "Emma, first I felt terrible sadness, then the greatest happiness ever, and now horrible sadness, again. This cycle is unbearable."

Ironically, Emma was relieved. There is no reasoning with people who have the too-happy part, just to talk a bit, but most importantly, to have them drink the healing water. When the wretchedness returns, one can explain the situation.

"My love, most people who become truly sad just stay that way till they get treated, though immediate help is crucial, as they may have feelings of not wanting to live that can take them into really dark places; that condition is quite common. Some need to take medicines, speak to a talk medical doctor, and have a caring companion. Most of them don't even need all that, after they improve, and some don't need all that even during their extreme sadness. Your case is rarer and much more complex, not to mention that regular talk medical doctors are helpless against it."

"So, what will become of me?"

"If you comply with the treatment, contentment can be sustained, most of the time. The salt water remedy I put in the orange juice treats the Too Happy–Too Sad disorder. It's a serious illness, and, when it's untreated, it gets people in a lot of trouble, including getting locked up forever. That's what makes your case riskier than just extreme sadness. When one turns to the too-happy part, the danger is greater, because being violent affects those around them in more severe ways. And unlike the extreme sadness, you must do the treatment, indefinitely, or you'll get sick again—no exceptions, ever!

"And Tim, I'd *never* listen to anybody who says you're just ordinary. Overcoming that uncommon illness makes a person unique, and, of course, you've *always* been special to me, and that's all I care about."

"Thank you, Emma. So, I'll do the treatment, and when I get better, we'll plan the next stage of our lives."

"That's a very responsible and realistic plan, and makes people with your malady get, and stay, better. Now, shower, groom, and let's grab some breakfast." After that, they went to the pond, the lake, and the cherry orchard, and they did everything that worked before. This went on for about two more months.

Chapter 17: Tim Gets Well and Revisiting the Meadow

When he turned contented again, Emma was 20 and Tim was 19. That afternoon, there was a knock on the hut's door.

"Coming."

Tim stood there, smiling and happy, but not overly happy.

She jumped into his arms and they embraced and kissed for a long while, as though making up for lost time. "I've wanted to do this for a whole year. Do you realize how hard it was for me to hold back?" said Emma

Tim had tears of joy. "Emma, you removed my suffering with your caring, talks, games, and the special salty water. It's like in fairy tales, when the prince breaks the spell by kissing the princess."

"There's one big difference. The princess didn't make any effort, and then one day, the prince just appeared out of nowhere and saved her. You worked *really* hard for this Tim, and I'm so proud of you. I don't know how you view yourself—Tim—but to me, you're a hero. But, my love, I've missed you so much. I want us to go to our meadow again. Are you up to it?"

"My thoughts and emotions were garbled for a whole year. But it's all over now. Let's go and become one again."

They went to the meadow, joyfully. A group of bright yellow canaries flew above. Tim picked a poppy, and put it in Emma's hair, who looked more beautiful than ever. Then, among the flowers, they made passionate love.

Chapter 18: Tim's Concerns and Emma's Reassurances

The next day, Tim came to visit Emma.

"So, what's next? We have to tell your parents."

"Emma, please give me your hand," said Tim confidently.

Tim had some apprehensions, though. He lived his entire life in the palace, in a sheltered manner, and lacked many life, work, social, and interpersonal skills. *How will Emma react, when, not if, things go awry*? he thought, and he shared those fears with her.

"Oh, Tim, I know what I'm getting myself into. Marriage is not always 50–50. Only Trust and Faithfulness have to be equal. Someone from your social background, and with your illness, will definitely have challenges. Just keep drinking the well water, and keep the lines of communication open with me.

"There's a talking medical doctor in the capital, named Dr. Robin, who charges a lot from the wealthy, and a little from the poor. He's compassionate, thoughtful, and very effective.

"Decent employment can be found and handled. Once I teach a life skill, you'll be more independent, and we can do things together, or divide jobs according to our abilities.

"What amazes me most, Tim, is that through humility, you knew from a young age that living a regular life and being friends with me—a simple peasant girl—was all that you desired."

"Thank you, Emma," said Tim, teary-eyed, not quite knowing how to follow such a testament of caring, love, and self-sacrifice.

They walked till they reached the palace.

Chapter 19: The Confrontation with Tim's Parents

They both entered the palace, and walked into the grand dining room. The king and queen were eating, although on opposite sides of a long, drab, wooden table, without a table cloth. Maybe the queen was saving for retirement.

"Marra, would you like some more meat?"

"If I wanted more, I would have asked the servant," she said scornfully.

"I am just trying to be nice."

"What do you want from me?!"

"Nothing. Just forget all about it."

"Forgotten!"

The king kept his eyes on the plate. Even he was scared of the queen—at least for now.

Suddenly, they looked, in shock, at Emma and Tim, who were quietly observing this entire scene. One could hear a fork drop.

"What is going on here? What are you doing with that helper?" asked the queen, repulsed.

"Father, Mother, this is my girlfriend—Emma."

"You know that the kingdom's rules are that the prince cannot associate with peasants, and certainly not have one as a girlfriend. And anyway, how did she end up being your companion? I am totally confused," said the king.

"When I needed assistance, and you put up the posters, Emma saw one, and came to help right away, like good girlfriend would," fibbed Tim. "And, anyway, I *never* wanted to be a prince or the king. My brother Cornelius can take the throne."

Cornelius was listening the entire time, from another room, with glee. *I knew Tim was never king material. It would be great to be the ruler and exercise unconstrained power over our people, to control the kingdoms we already own, with ruthlessness, and to conquer new nations. I, especially, want to make the Western Islanders' life more miserable—I really hated that Johnnie.*

"Emma and I want to get married in a civil union, not by the church of the kingdom. We will live outside the palace, independently. But, please come to the wedding."

That was the moment when the queen could not take it anymore. "We gave you everything: life, a palace, fancy food, and servants— how ungrateful you are. You roguishly lied to us for nine years, and fraternized with a filthy, low-life, peasant. What do you even see in her?!"

Emma looked at Tim, concerned. But, a gentle and reassuring squeeze warmed her cold and scared hand.

And Tim's words reached King James' ears, and his judgment and wrath came on quickly. "Tim sees in Emma what he never saw in you. And she sees in him what you never even tried to see in him."

"Oh James, how *dare* you?"

"Because I made the same mistakes myself, but no more! Tim is my son, and Emma is a good woman, and you will not speak to them that way. He has been through enough, and she risked her life for him, which just makes your callous words worse."

"You will have to choose: me, or that…that…scoundrel."

"Marra, won't you reconsider?"

"No!"

"In that case, I choose my son. I will not allow you to instill fear in me, nor hurt Tim, ever again."

The queen stormed out of the dining room, and she told her mother Eva about the king's change of heart. Both the queen and her mother, who remained remorseless as well, packed up their things, and took a ferry to the mainland. A poor chap of a king, recently widowed, and who thought little of himself, married

her, immediately.

Chapter 20: Tim's Father Comes Around, and There is Forgiveness

"Tim," said King James contritely, "I am so sorry for *never* being a good father, and treating you like one of my soldiers or servants. Even my initial assistance when you became bedridden was aggressive, just like I always treated you."

"But Father, you did get me medical help, and Emma's help too. As far as the rest—let us leave it behind."

The king nodded solemnly, with gratitude. "And look at you, Emma, my loving and beautiful soon-to-be daughter-in-law, who saved my son's life, and put all the noblemen's and my king friends' daughters to shame. How wrong I was about non-royal people."

"Your Majesty, it is fine."

"No it is not. And please call me Father."

"Father, I forgive you."

"Thank you. If you two want to lead a simple, happy life outside the palace, and you want to be financially independent, then you have my blessing. We can always visit each other."

"You can visit us, but we will not be coming here. I just want to forget about this place and start a fresh new life."

"I understand. I would like to at least offer you a wedding gift."

Chapter 21: The Requests—Tim's Transformation

Tim's eyes lit up, and he said, "We have four requests, and that is the only gift needed. First: Please issue an edict that not only would permit girls and women to read and use the library, but *encourage* them to do so, and especially in schools.

"Two: Mr. Brook, the librarian, is about to retire, and he said that Emma is most qualified to take over. It could be her employment.

"Three: Please issue the strongest warning to the males in our kingdom, to protect females' physical safety, and treat them respectfully.

"Finally, please pass a law prohibiting financial penalties, work without pay for the kingdom, arbitrary conscription to the army, and punishment or imprisonment for peasants and all non-royalty—that is, when there is no wrongdoing."

"It will take some time to implement, but I will start working on it immediately. Is there any material gift that you want for yourselves?"

"No, thank you. Please, just grant what we asked for, and come to the wedding."

"It would be my pleasure. Where will you live?"

"At Emma's mother's hut, along with her mother, until we can afford our own place. The wedding will be next Thursday, by the capital's court, at 6:09 in the evening, exactly."

"I will be there."

Chapter 22: Who Will Be the Next King?

"And please listen, Tim," continued the king, "Cornelius—that cold, narcissistic, argumentative, browbeating, and pigheaded brother of yours—will *never* be the next king. I will buy him a full-size mirror for his next birthday, and after he completes the school of higher education, he will have to support himself."

"My cousin Frank and I both have our grandfather, the deceased king, as a patriarch, so that means Frank qualifies as an heir. Being noble and meek are desirable assets to inheriting the throne. After your requests are followed, I'll retire immediately. He will become King, and lead us into a new era of Justice and Peace.

"Tim, I envy you; all the lands, money, and power did not give me true love and happiness. And it was humility that showed you the way."

Chapter 23: The Queen's, her Mother's, and Cornelius' Bitter End

Cornelius immediately got on a ferry and joined Eva, Marra, and her new poor bloke of a king husband, and he was a brat over there, too. Good riddance!

However, the mirror in the new palace got tired of his vain staring marathons, and one day, it swallowed him whole. The only thing that remained was an image etched in the looking glass, instead of a soul, for Cornelius had none to begin with. Since that was the only remnant of her only beloved son, the former queen took very good care of the mirror.

But, both mother and daughter made the king's life miserable, and he expelled them both, along with the mirror. She went from king to king, just being herself, and developed an ill reputation on the mainland.

The last king she ended up with locked all three up in a high tower, not to protect them from the world, but the other way around.

And one day, having no one else to abuse and torment, both daughter and mother turned on each other and had the ultimate yelling and hitting match, and all three fell out of the window into their death, as even the mirror containing Cornelius' picture shattered into smithereens.

Chapter 24: Murdoch's Bitterer End

Uncle Murdoch was petrified. He was five years older than Tim at the time of the crime, and that age disparity constituted a bona fide legal infraction. Hurting a royal family member was punishable by being hung on a tree.

He heard that a few years earlier, a huge new mainland was discovered after crossing the Great Western Sea. Murdoch, the abuser, found out that the inhabitants, who were pure people, were tricked into exchanging gold in return for worthless plastic knickknacks. He planned to do the same.

He boarded the next ship headed there. But his awful sense of humor did not ring well with the longshoremen, and, as their esprit de corps was deteriorating, they threw him overboard along with those darn trinkets.

And till today, the bauble bag and Murdoch's remains still float somewhere in that Great Western Sea, because plastic floats and so does that smelly, nasty stuff that comes out of the human body after you eat food.

Chapter 25: The Hug

Tim and Emma embraced. They cried tears of joy, excitement, and Hope, but also of a lot of pain—pain of everything they had gone through since they first met on the trail—on the day that changed their lives, and the lives of everyone in the entire kingdom, forever.

Chapter 26: The Wedding

The wedding was a simple civil ceremony. The magistrate, who was an old friend of Emma's father's before he died, performed it at no cost. King James, and Emma's mother attended, nicely dressed. Afterwards, there was a modest party in the small back yard of Emma's mother's hut, along with two of Emma's girlfriends. They served roasted chicken, roasted potatoes, and tall glasses of freshly squeezed orange juice.

And they both lived happily ever after—but *not* in the palace.

THE END

Biography

Peter D. Weiler writes from West Los Angeles, California. Because he has suffered from bipolar disorder and other psychiatric and mental conditions himself for many years, he has a soft spot for others who suffer. He has written over 70 short stories—mostly love stories—about an individual with disorders who has improved and recovered. The common motif in his work is: No matter how isolated, mentally ill, or downtrodden you are, you can always find Health, Love, and Hope.

He is currently working on his next fable, *The Terrified Prince.* Watch for other books to come in this series.

Peter loves to make people laugh, because when you're beset by tremendous challenges, humor makes navigating through life a lot easier.

73

Made in the USA
San Bernardino, CA
17 November 2018